The Guests

Guests

The

Courtship

The Honeymoon

moon

The Proposal

Proposal

The Courtship

The Wedding

For love bugs everywhere

This popular song was first recorded more than four hundred

years ago as *The Wedding of the Frogge and the Mouse.*

Over the years, singers have changed words and added many new verses.

Similarly, this version borrows from traditional sources, with new words added along the way.

It can be read as verse or sung. To sing it, read the first line of the couplet

through once and add "Um–hum! Um–hum!" at the end.

Then sing the entire couplet and add "Um–hum! Um–hum!" afterward.

And remember, it's fun to add verses of your own too!

Especially Dar

Card Number 2004045170. ISBN 0–7636–2306–7 Printed in China This book was typeset in Dickens. The illustrations were done in watercolor and ink.
Candlewick Press, 2067 Massachusetts Avenue, Cambridge, Massachusetts 02140. visit us at www.candlewick.com 10 9 8 7 6 5 4 3 2 1

Froggy Went A-Courtin'

CANDLEWICK PRESS
CAMBRIDGE, MASSACHUSETTS

Gillian Tyler

The Courtship

Froggy went a-courtin' and he did ride,

Sword and pistol by his side.

He rode up to Miss Mousie's door,
Where he had often been before.

"Oh, Miss Mouse, are you within?"
"Yes, kind frog, I sit and spin."

The Proposal

He took Miss Mousie on his knee,
Said, "Miss Mouse, will you marry me?"

" Without asking my Uncle Rat,
I could not say yes to that!"

And Uncle Rat, when he came home,
Said, "Who's been here since I've been gone?"

"A handsome gentleman," said she,
"Who says he wants to marry me."

Um ~ hum
Um ~ hum

"Where will the wedding breakfast be?"

"Way down yonder in the hollow tree."

"What will the wedding breakfast be?"

"Three green beans and a black-eyed pea."

"Who will make the wedding gown?"

"I'll have one made for me in town."

Then Uncle Rat gave his consent . . .

And here's
the way
the wedding
went.

The Wedding

The first to come in was a little white moth;

She spread out the tablecloth.

Um-hum! Um-hum!

Next to come in was a Juney bug;

On his back was a root beer jug.

Next to come in was a turtledove,

Who brought the bride and groom her love.

Next to come in was a garter snake,

Helped himself to the wedding cake.

Next to come in was a bumblebee,
Played the banjo on his knee.

Um - hum! Um - hum!

Next to come in was a nimble flea,
Danced a jig for the bumblebee.

Next to come in were the fancy ants,
Stepping out in a floral dance.

The last to come in was Mister Fly,

Didn't get one piece of pie.

Then the old tomcat came tumbling in

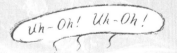

And put an end to the merrymakin'.

The Honeymoon

The frog and the mouse went to France,
And that's the end of this romance.

The Happy Ending

Their wedding album is laid on the shelf —
If you want any more, you can sing it yourself!

Um-hum!

The Courtship   The Proposal   The Wedding

The Proposal   The Wedding   The

The Proposal   The Wedding   The Guests

The Wedding   The Guests   The Honey

Wedding   The Guests   The Honeymoon